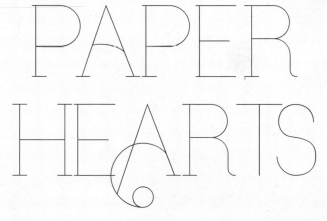

PAPER
HEARTS

With thanks, to Edward

— SANDRA

Published in 2014 by Simply Read Books · www.simplyreadbooks.com
Text & illustrations © 2014 Sandra Van Doorn

Library and Archives Canada Cataloguing in Publication

Van Doorn, Sandra
    Paper hearts / written and illustrated by Sandra Van Doorn.

ISBN 978-1-927018-41-5
    I. Title.
PZ7.V275Pa 2014 j823'.92 C2013-901263-X

Manufactured in Malaysia

Book design by Robin Mitchell Cranfield for hundreds & thousands

We gratefully acknowledge for their financial support of our publishing program
the Canada Council for the Arts, the BC Arts Council, and the Government of
Canada through the Canada Book Fund (CBF).

10 9 8 7 6 5 4 3 2 1

SANDRA VAN DOORN

PAPER HEARTS

SIMPLY READ BOOKS

All day long, I sit at the window
and watch people walking by.

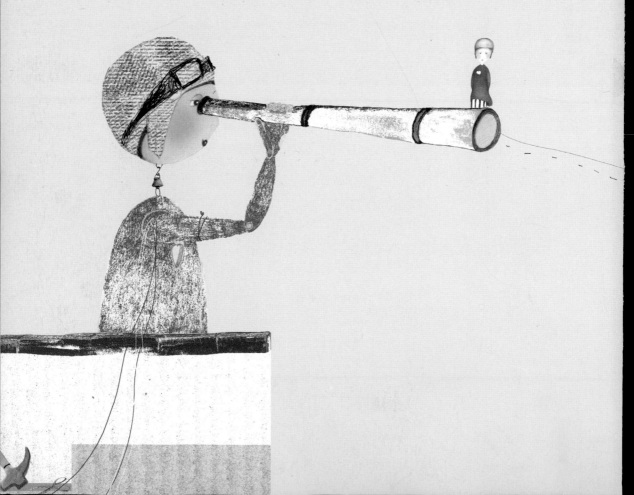

Some walk hand in hand.
Some stop to hug and kiss.
They are all busy with a funny thing called

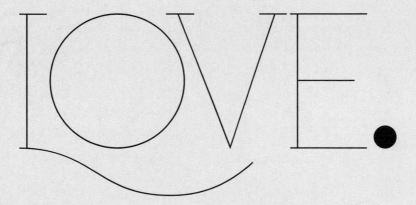

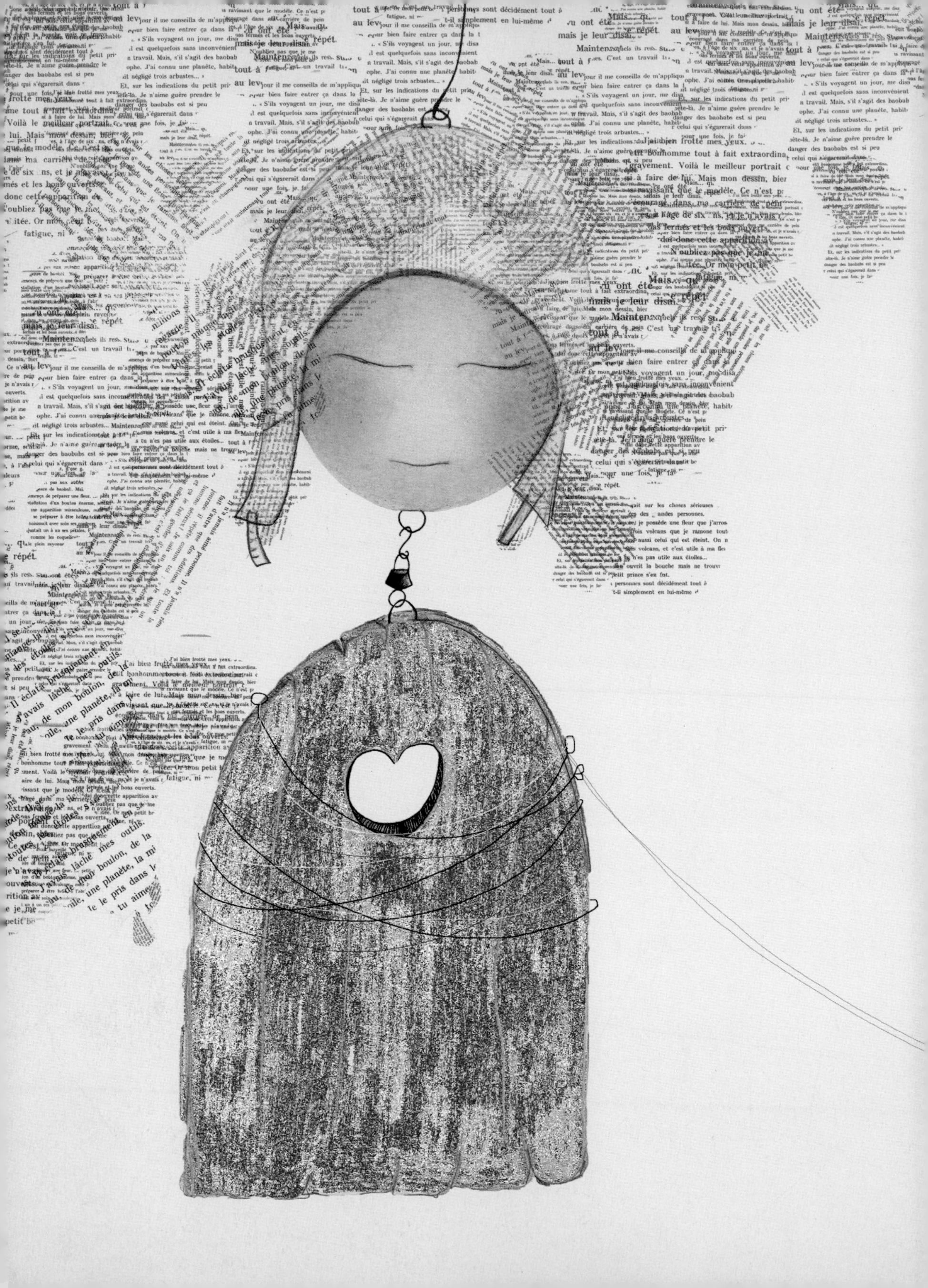

But I don't feel anything.
I am just a puppet.
I wonder what it feels like, love…
If only I had a

HEART,

I would know.

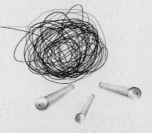

Perhaps I can make one out of

PAPER.

As I cut it out, I realize…

...paper hearts say
beautiful things
without ever speaking,
like

SWEET NOTES

without words.

Paper hearts come in all sorts of colors,
like the color of friendship, secrets, laughs
and sometimes tears, eternal summers,
and pure

HAPPINESS.

Paper hearts love to flutter,
just like

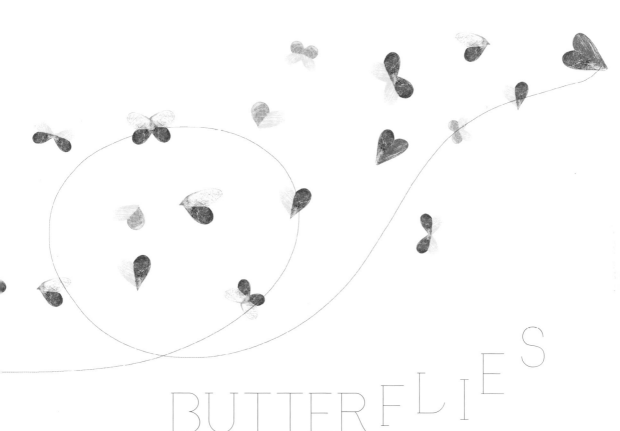

BUTTERFLIES

in your tummy.

Paper hearts are light and happy,
so light they can get swept

AWAY...

Paper hearts can also fall,
like

FALLING

head over heels.

Paper hearts can
be given
to someone special,
even in

SECRET.

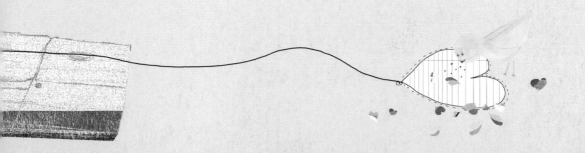

Et j'aime la nuit écouter les étoiles.

And they can be stolen, which is not really nice.
But they can be

FOUND

again, somewhere least expected.

Just like real hearts, paper hearts are fragile.
And if you are not careful,

they can be

TORN.

But you can put them back together and
patch them up.

Although they are never quite the same,
just like real hearts.

Paper hearts are all so different
in their own beautiful ways.
And I realize that torn, patched up,

CRINKLED,

happy and colorful…

...my paper heart is

It is just like a real heart to me.

I will find someone I know to keep my
heart safe and